BARRAMUNDI TRIANGLE

CAROLYN DENMAN

Barramundi Triangle by Carolyn Denman
© Copyright 2016 Carolyn Denman

This is a work of fiction. Names, characters, businesses, places, events and incidents are either the products of the author's imagination or used in a fictitious manner. Any resemblance to actual persons, living or dead, or actual events is purely coincidental.

Website: carolyndenman.com
Email: carolyn@carolyndenman.com
Facebook: Carolyn J Denman

Good Reads: Carolyn Denman

Twitter: on CDenmanAuthor

ISBN: 978-0-9953601-0-5

First Print: August 2016

Chapter 1

A cloud of black smoke filled the shed, accompanied by a sound that was not even remotely similar to that of a happily humming engine. In fact, it sounded more like a drowning kookaburra.

'Don't rev it so hard. It'll only flood,' I suggested as I shoved the mess of tools aside with my foot. There was, after all, a slim chance that the dirt bike might actually make it outdoors at some point and it would need a clear path to get there.

'It sounds more like it isn't getting *enough* petrol,' Nicole said, waving her hands around to disperse the smoke. 'Turn it off before something catches fire.' But her comments only made her brother rev it more.

The bike shuddered and made a few knocking noises, and spat out another fat puff of dirty exhaust. Then it began to purr.

'Yeah, baby, come on,' Noah coaxed it, wheeling it carefully forward like it was a trolley full of egg cartons. 'Lainie, could you please move the sump bucket out of the way?'

I did, and he almost made it to the door before it started coughing again, and this time when he revved it, it screamed, bucked, and cut out with a petulant bang. I knew he'd flood it.

I wiped my oily hands on my jeans. 'Want me to go and ask your mum for help?'

'She's not home, and anyway, I can fix it myself,' Noah insisted. 'I helped Caleb fix the pump for the top dam and that thing is about three years older than Adam.'

He sounded just like his dad when he used that phrase.

'Yeah, but that was a diesel engine,' I said.

'So?'

I sighed. 'Nothing. Just try it again. I'm sure all it needs is another six or seven attempts without actually fixing anything and it will just miraculously start to work. Have you noticed that the back tyre is flat?'

Nicole jumped down from her vantage point up on the tractor and followed us out of the shed. 'This is boring. I'm going to check on Curly. I reckon she's dropped and she'll lamb today.'

Curly was a ewe that Nicole had raised as an orphaned lamb. How Nicole could even tell which one Curly was amongst the other sixty or so sheep in the same paddock was beyond me. In fact, my guess was that she couldn't. She was only eight years old but loved to pretend that she knew everything there was about farming. Her favourite trick was to announce when each ewe was due to lamb and then brag about it when a new baby appeared. It didn't seem to matter if it was the wrong ewe that had dropped. Today Curly would be whichever ewe was next to produce a sparkly white bundle of wool.

'I should probably go too,' I told Noah. 'Aunt Lily wants me to help her clear out the small hay shed.' I retied my long hair back into some semblance of its original plait. The residual oil left on my fingers made it a bit easier than usual.

Noah sat back on his heels, poking at the back tyre as if that would help him assess how much pressure was in it. 'What for? It's the wrong time of year for cutting hay.'

'Apparently we're buying in some extra from a contractor in Bridgewater. Harry's done some deal with him and got a good price. He reckons we won't have enough from our cut.'

'Righto. Did you want a hand?'

My eyes narrowed. What thirteen-year-old boy offers to spend a sunny Sunday afternoon helping clean out his neighbour's hay shed? Normally he'd be trying to pester Liam and Caleb into letting him tag along with whatever they were doing. 'Where are your brothers?'

He looked up at me from under his long blond eyelashes. His green eyes were overly innocent. 'Mum took them to Horsham to buy clothes for their school formal. She threatened to dress them the same if they didn't come and choose something.'

'So what are you supposed to be doing while they're gone?' I asked.

'Homework.'

'We don't have any,' I said. 'Do we?' Maybe I'd missed something.

'That assignment on Nalong's Dreaming stories.'

'That was due nearly two weeks ago,' I said. He blinked at me, uncaring, and I rolled my eyes. 'Just get it done, Noah. I've already given you my notes.'

4

'Harry said they're wrong. He told me some extra things to put in.'

'And what would a farmhand know about writing an English essay?'

Noah frowned at me but I ignored him. Harry was not in my good books.

'You're still mad at him for not giving that newspaper clipping back,' he guessed.

I nodded.

'Can your aunt talk to him?'

'She won't. She says I'm overreacting.'

'I don't blame her. You're totally bonkers.' He opened the petrol cap to check the level. 'Hey, this is empty,' he announced brightly. 'No wonder!'

Two minutes later he was tearing up chunks of grass and mud as he gave his new hand-me-down dirt bike a spin in the first paddock that was out of sight from the house.

Chapter 2

It was Friday and school was finished but we were stuck in town for at least another half hour, waiting on Noah's mum. She'd offered to drive us home from school instead of taking the bus because she was picking up their ride-on mower, which had just been repaired from when Liam had rolled it. He was banned from using it now but he didn't mind because it got him out of having to cut the grass. The mower was ready to go but the Ashbree's trailer lights had blown a fuse in their car so Mrs Ashbree had gone to buy a new one. Noah had been left at the mechanic's to mind the mower while I'd ducked over a couple of streets to the centre of town.

'Where have you been?' Noah asked as I dumped my school bag at his feet.

'Library. Mrs Hamilton doesn't believe me.'

'What did you tell her?' Noah asked me.

'The usual. I said I had a school assignment on organised crime and needed to see the newspaper records.'

Noah laughed. 'Right. Because organised crime is an important part of what we have to study in Year 8. Can't you just look it up on the internet?'

'Don't you think I haven't tried? It happened back in 1992 so the only thing I have to go on is that one newspaper clipping I found in our study. Harry only let me read half of it before he snatched it away. Why did he have to pick that moment to come in to ask Aunt Lily about the hay contract? The stupid clipping must have been in our study for years. He had to come in just when I came across it.'

'Are you sure it mentioned your mum's name?'

I glared at him. 'I might not remember much about Mum but I haven't forgotten her name, Noah.'

'All right, no need to get shirty with me. I just think it's a bit of a long shot that your mum had anything to do with the famous Nalong drugs bust.'

'It wasn't a drugs bust. It was about some diamonds. That's why they killed her.'

'Who, your mum? I thought she – '

'Not Mum, you idiot! The woman whose body they never found.'

Noah shook his head as he climbed onto the mower and rested his long legs up on the steering wheel. He was growing so tall that he would probably be called on to take over Liam's mowing chores if he could push the clutch down far enough. Whenever I tried it, I had to sit so far forward that I triggered the dead man's switch under the seat, and the engine cut out.

'You have got to stop believing the stupid stories that Tori McKenzie tells you,' he said. 'She also reckons drinking from the river will make you fall pregnant, remember? There's no dead body out in the state park.'

'I bet there is. You could hide anything out there. Even treasure.'

'Like diamonds?' he scoffed. 'Rubbish.'

'Then why did the owner of the jewellery store get arrested at the same time as those other two men?'

'You said he was released.'

'Yeah, but his shop closed down.'

'So?'

Noah was so annoying sometimes.

'Lainie, where are you going?'

'Back to the library,' I called over my shoulder. 'I'll wait until Mrs Hamilton is distracted and then look at the papers myself. I need to know what happened, Noah.'

'Whatever,' he said. 'Just get back before Mum does. If she has to bail you out of trouble she'll be late picking up Liam and Caleb from basketball and then there'll be hell to pay.'

***

'I'm sorry, Lainie, but the last time I let school kids look at the newspapers, they were left in a complete mess and some of them were ripped. Why do you really want to see them?' Mrs Hamilton looked at me through her trendy red glasses. They looked out of place on such a wrinkled face. Far too funky to be worn with that plastic chain around her neck. And she was on to me now. No chance of sneaking past her. I was going to have to resort to a horribly dirty tactic.

'My dad's accident. I want to read the report,' I said. My nervous expression wasn't even fake. If there was one thing I didn't want to see, it was that report. Aunt Lily had told me enough. Too much.

As expected, Mrs Hamilton melted. I hoped she wasn't going to try to hug me because she reeked of Jennifer Lopez perfume. It was the same perfume Noah's aunt had bought me for my birthday last year. I didn't like it.

'Perhaps you should talk to someone instead,' she suggested with soft eyes. 'Your aunt – '

The double doors of the library opened as someone left, and the sound of a small engine distracted everyone's attention. Someone was driving on the pavement outside, and getting closer. A flash of red. Oh my Great Grandmother. What was he doing?

I mumbled a quick thanks that Mrs Hamilton didn't hear and moved away from the desk. She barely glanced at me before striding over to the doors so she could yell at the person making such a racket near her quiet reading sanctuary.

Noah got to the doors before she did, pushing them open with the bumper bar of the mower and nearly bowling her over. He was singing a song from the school production that he'd been roped into earlier in the year. Everyone had said that he'd made a very impressive Joseph in his Dreamcoat, despite his voice. He certainly captured everyone's attention this time. Mowers are particularly loud when they're indoors, surrounded by offended office staff. There were only half-height partitions between the library space and council office workers' desks.

It took me less than three minutes to find and read the clipping I was after. I'd seen the date on the one Harry had confiscated, and Mrs Hamilton kept them in meticulous order. By the time I'd tidied up and snuck out the side door, the wail of a police siren was adding to the disruption of the usually silent room. Noah was in so much trouble. For me. I tried to wave at him through the window to tell him he could stop, but he couldn't see me because the room was filled with exhaust and flying papers. There was a lot of shouting, and then some clever person decided it would be a good idea to try to block his path with a book trolley. Its wheels made a hideous sound as he pushed it along with the mower.

I sighed. Apparently his legs were long enough for the clutch now after all. Which meant that his list of Saturday chores just got a whole lot longer.

Chapter 3

The river didn't seem to care how much trouble we were in. It just kept singing its way past us as we sat on our favourite rocks in the little sandy curve below my house. I broke off a piece of stick and threw it as far across the water as I could and then watched as it was swallowed, becoming part of the river itself, sweeping out of the home paddock and bending southwards before following the road towards town. Everything was part of the river really. Everything it touched became part of its journey, its identity. A complex, evolving, living thing.

'Remember the last boat I built?' Noah asked, staring into the water as well. 'The raft I tied together with about a million pieces of hay band? It would have worked.'

Seriously? He was still hung up on that? It was over two years ago. 'Yeah, I remember. It was against the rules. Hay band isn't naturally found in the bush. Harry's original challenge was supposed to be about bush craft. You're the one that wanted to turn it into a competition to see who could make a boat that would survive all the way from your place to here.'

'I just want to know why it's so hard,' Noah said. 'I'm telling you, there's something weird going on out there in the state park. Creepy ghosts or evil spirits or something. Maybe that's why Harry won't tell you about what happened out there with your mum. He knows all the ancient legends.'

'The Barramundi Triangle,' we said together, laughing. I had accidentally used the wrong word years ago after one of my own rafts had failed to turn up – I'd been trying to say it was like the Bermuda Triangle, but got it wrong.

'If there are ghosts out there, then my parents would be with them,' I said. 'They wouldn't be creepy or evil.'

He acknowledged that by not arguing back. We watched a leafy branch float past, spinning where it passed our rocks.

'I'm sorry I got you into trouble,' Noah said after a few moments. 'They didn't believe me.' He actually sounded surprised.

I chucked the rest of my stick at him. 'You said someone dared you to do it. Who did you expect them to blame?'

He chucked it straight back, hitting me in the thigh. 'Ben Millard was in the library, and I tried to imply it had been him, but then he told them he saw you nick something from behind the counter.'

'What? I didn't steal anything! I didn't even tear out the clipping, even though I wanted to. He's such a pain.'

I tore the stick into little pieces and threw them as hard as I could into the water. Why were all the kids at school so mean to me? They all seemed to like Noah no matter what he did.

'I should have thought it through better. Sorry.'

'It's okay. Was totally worth it. And I can't believe you did that for me.'

Noah sat up straighter. 'I thought you said the clipping was useless.'

I smiled sideways at him. 'Not entirely. The only mention of my mum was that she was "assisting police with their enquiries" and I was hoping for more, but there are other clues. I was right that the three men had links to a crime gang. I think one of them was the boss of the other two. He ordered them to murder the woman. Or maybe she knew where the diamonds were and wouldn't tell them, so they killed her.'

'The newspaper actually talked about diamonds? I thought Tori was making that bit up.'

'It mentioned an earlier attack on a guy named William Lewis. They reckon they were fighting over a jewellery theft. Also there was the owner of the jewellery store involved, remember?'

'That doesn't mean there are diamonds,' Noah argued. 'Could have just been a pretty necklace or something. Some family heirloom, worth peanuts.'

I rolled my eyes. 'Noah, William Lewis died from his injuries, and a woman was murdered. That doesn't happen over peanuts.'

'I dunno. I'm pretty hungry right now. I'd murder you over some peanuts. How much longer do you think they'll be talking? Mum will need to take Nicole to footy soon. She has practice matches every Saturday arvo for the next few weeks.'

We both looked up the hill towards my house where Noah's mum and my aunt were 'having a chat' with the police sergeant. Aunt Lily had told us to go outside for a while and Noah's mum had said to stay close. Sergeant Loxwood had just ignored us. I'd had to drag Noah away from playing in the shiny blue and white police Landcruiser while we waited. He seemed to think he could do anything he wanted without anyone getting mad at him. Probably because it was usually true. His big green eyes always looked so innocent that most grown-ups forgot what they were telling him off for as soon as he smiled at them. I didn't think that was likely to work on the policeman though.

I was just about to suggest that we listen in outside the window when the door opened and Harry walked out. The farmhand didn't even glance around first. He looked straight over to where we were and waved at us to come in. He knew where all our favourite spots were.

'When did Harry get back?' Noah asked, standing up. 'I thought you said he was out fixing a leak in one of the water troughs.'

I shrugged. 'I guess he finished.'

'I think he's sneaky. He's always turning up where we don't expect him.'

I laughed as I raced him up the embankment. 'You only think that because he always catches us when we go somewhere we're not supposed to be. Like that time we nicked the Nutella jar and climbed on the machinery shed roof to eat it.'

'But we were so quiet! And he couldn't possibly have seen us through the trees. He's way too nosy for a farmhand. Why is he getting involved in this, anyway?'

Harry was still waiting on the doorstep. He looked like he could wait there all day. He never looked impatient, and was never cross. He was, however, a master of that facial expression that said he was disappointed in us and that we'd somehow let him down. Noah always seemed more worried about being on the receiving end of that than he was about the growling and yelling that he got from his mum. By the time we reached the house, the expression was out in full force, but Harry didn't say a word. We followed him in.

Sergeant Loxwood was sitting with the others around the kitchen table, drinking coffee. There was a plate of scones in front of him but he hadn't taken any. No one had. Not one crumb or drip of cream had sullied any of the little saucers I'd handed out earlier. Must have been a serious chat.

I took an apple from the bowl on the microwave and sat down while Noah grabbed a saucer and piled three scones onto it before reaching for the jam.

The sergeant watched him coolly, waiting until he had a mouthful of cream before speaking. 'Mrs Hamilton has persuaded her manager not to press charges against either of you for yesterday's debacle.' He looked right into my eyes. 'She seems to be under the impression that you, Lainie, might be in need of some counselling and that Noah was somehow "just trying to be a good friend". I have no idea why she would think that, do you?'

For a moment I was utterly confused, but then remembered I had been asking to see the report on my dad's accident. She must have thought Noah was trying to help me get a look at it. Mrs Hamilton was much smarter than I'd assumed. Could I pretend this was all about the fact that my parents were dead? Get the sympathy vote? A quick glance at my aunt's face dispelled that idea. She would be devastated, and sit on the end of my bed every night until I fell asleep, just in case I wanted to talk about things I really didn't want to talk about.

'Noah *is* a good friend,' I told the sergeant. 'He just takes things too far sometimes.'

Sergeant Loxwood looked meaningfully at Noah's mum with a silent 'I told you so'.

Two grey paws appeared at the edge of the table where the cat was reaching up to investigate where the dripped cream had come from. Noah pushed her off the chair. 'I really am sorry I did it. I didn't think it would cause so much disruption. It just seemed like a funny thing to do, waking everyone up.'

'No one was sleeping, Noah,' his mum berated. 'They were working. Quietly. You left mud tracks everywhere, and the place still smells like the pits at Winton Racecourse.'

'It's not like I put the blades down or anything,' he mumbled.

The sergeant stood up. 'Six weeks of community service, Noah. You'll help out at St Peter's op shop for four hours every Saturday morning, and then clean the library windows. Lainie, you will spend this Sunday helping the Horsham Girl Guides to pick up rubbish and plant trees.'

Nooo! Not those snobby townies! I wouldn't mind if they actually did any work, but all they ever did was walk around gossiping all day. Then it dawned on me.

'Wait, did you say this Sunday? I can't,' I said around a mouthful of apple. 'It's the Tatura Show. I'm jumping that day and there's a new horse I'm having a look at. They're bringing Buddy all the way up from Melbourne so I can try him out.'

12

Aunt Lily glared at me. 'Lainie, you do not have the authority to argue with a police officer. You'll do whatever he tells you to do!'

Noah slid his saucer across the table to my aunt, offering her a scone and a dimpled smile. 'Ms Gracewood, I can do Lainie's punishment for her. She didn't do anything wrong. She's been training for ages for this show.'

From the look on her face it almost seemed to work, for about half a second, until Harry cleared his throat and caught my eye. 'I think you've gotten each other into enough trouble already. The last thing Noah needs is to spend a day with a bunch of Girl Guides.'

He was right. Those Barbie dolls would go nuts competing for his attention. Noah would hate it even more than I would. I couldn't do that to him. I flopped my cheek down onto the table and let out a massive sigh. 'I'll call Buddy's owners and tell them I can't make it. You're right, Aunt Lily. Sergeant Loxwood is the boss of this town and I should do what he says. He found and caught those murderers on the southern fire trail all those years ago. If he hadn't, there'd be a bunch of murderers still living in the state park and you'd never let me ride in there.'

Silent questions filled the kitchen while all the adults looked over to Harry, of all people. Then the sergeant frowned at me, so I sat up again and gave him a feeble smile. He put his coffee mug in the sink and then sat down again.

'Are you afraid of strangers out in the park? Have you seen anything that might make you worried?' he asked me.

I sat up slowly, but didn't meet his gaze, and didn't speak.

'Lainie, if you've seen anything at all, you have to let me know. Or are you just worried because you've heard stories about what happened to your mum all those years ago?'

My head snapped up just as Aunt Lily gasped. Noah got in first.

'Did they ever find the diamonds?' he asked quickly, almost bouncing out of his chair.

Harry placed a hand on his shoulder and replied before his mum could tell him off. 'There were no diamonds. It was a misunderstanding. Those men were evil and the police dealt with them and now they're gone.' His voice was soothing, sensible, but I needed more.

'What happened to my mum?' I demanded, looking at each one of them to see who would answer me.

'Nothing,' Harry said. 'She just helped lead the sergeant to the right place. Isn't that right, Mick?'

Sergeant Loxwood threw a quick glance at Aunt Lily, who shook her head slightly. He looked back at me. 'It's easy to get lost once you leave the tracks,' the policeman said. 'Your mum knew this area really well. I would have followed the river all the way back to town and never found the spot if your mum hadn't helped me.'

He was lying. Aunt Lily and Harry had just asked him to lie, and he had. Why?

A call came over his scanner. Something unintelligible to me but it didn't sound urgent.

'I need to get going,' the officer said. 'Noah, I'll let op shop volunteers know to expect you at 9am next Saturday morning. Make sure you're on time. Thanks for the coffee, Lily.' He rose and then nodded to Mrs Ashbree. 'There's just the matter of the carpet cleaner's bill, Sarah. I'll leave you to sort it out with Mrs Hamilton.'

'I'll drop Noah home and then head there right now,' she assured him. 'I have to take Nicole to footy anyway.'

Aunt Lily got up to see him out while Noah and I remained where we were, pinned by Mrs Ashbree's frown. As soon as we heard the police cruiser leave, she really let fly. By the time she was done I was quietly considering moving out to live in the bush as a hermit so I would never have to face her again, and Noah was promising to cut the grass every week for the rest of his life, now that his legs were apparently long enough to push the clutch all the way down.

Still, as they stood to leave a few minutes later, Noah threw me a sly smile.

14

Chapter 4

An hour later I found Harry staring out from his porch, gazing to the west as if he was trying to memorise every tree on the ridge. It looked like he'd been doing bookwork. There were bills and bank statements and sales catalogues strewn over the rickety outdoor table but he was leaning against his railing, ignoring it all and taking in the view instead. He seemed as restless as I was.

'Why won't you tell me what really happened?' I pestered, clutching at the rail as if to prevent him from dragging me away without answers.

'Because I don't want to scare you. The last thing any twelve-year-old needs is to have nightmares about murderers coming after their parents.' He turned to me with serious brown eyes. 'Nothing actually happened to your mum, I promise. She was fine. The men had a dispute with a local jeweller and she overheard them fighting. She did something brave and stupid to prevent them hurting the man and they turned on her, but your dad called the police and it all turned out fine. There were no diamonds, and no dead bodies hidden out in the bush. I've heard the crazy stories your friends tell each other. I knew you and Noah would turn the story into a big drama, which was why I didn't want you reading about it. Honestly, treasure hidden out in the bush?'

He squeezed my hand, and gave me such a soothing smile that I couldn't help but smile back. 'Yeah, that does sound a bit nuts.'

The wind picked up, scattering the leaves that had collected against the porch. Both of us looked over to the ridge, rising up on the other side of the river like a wall of green, trapping us in.

'So no one died?'

I waited, but only a lonely crow answered me. Harry was gripping the handrail and staring at the ridge.

'Harry?'

After a few more seconds he answered me, but didn't take his eyes from the skyline. 'There was a house fire the same day but stories have a way of getting mixed up. No one was murdered out in the bush.'

Aunt Lily always told me that I had an uncanny knack of being able to tell what people were thinking. I didn't think she was right, but I could tell that Harry knew the person who had died in that fire, and everything about the way he stood—so stiffly with his jaw tilted away from me—made it clear that he didn't want to talk about it, so I swallowed my curiosity.

'Was my mum really brave?' I asked instead.

He nodded. 'And stupid. She was a lot like you.'

I elbowed him hard and he laughed, and some of the tension seemed to leave his shoulders.

'I think you gave Sergeant Loxwood a bit of a fright today,' he said. 'Implying that you'd seen something out in the bush. He takes his job very seriously, as he should. I wouldn't be surprised if he left here and went for a drive to check out the area, just in case.'

'Just because of what I said? I never meant to imply I'd seen anything.'

'Yeah, I know. You were just fishing for confirmation about which fire trail they were caught on. The southern one, I think you mentioned?'

Far out, Harry was smart. I'd been hoping that mentioning a particular trail might have made one of them either confirm or deny it was the right one. It hadn't worked.

'It wasn't the southern one,' Harry said. 'The men were arrested miles from any track. Impossible to find without any landmarks or directions and there's nothing to see there anyway, so don't go doing anything stupid like trying to find the spot. Seriously no point.'

I let go of the railing feeling a bit let down. It wasn't like I'd been planning to go exploring out there or anything, but Noah would have loved the idea. Searching for treasure. Finding a skeleton and helping the police solve an old mystery. I was disappointed that there was no mystery to solve. My mum was gone, her story over, and I was never going to get to be a part of it, even as an epilogue. We'd just done an English assignment on epilogues. They were supposed to be the tidy bits at the end of a story. Happy endings. Like telling the readers that all the main characters had kids who ended up going to Hogwarts or ruling the Shire or finding the treasure and living happily ever after.

'I'd better make that phone call to Buddy's owners,' I said. 'I wouldn't want them to have to drive all that way for nothing. They should sell him to someone local.'

'Buddy is such a boring name for a horse anyway,' Harry said.

'I was going to rename him "Alonso". Much more fun.'

As I left, Harry almost looked sympathetic.

Chapter 5

The conversation with Harry had been bugging me all afternoon. No mysteries to be solved, no secrets to discover, but something was still off. My hot chocolate tasted terrible, for starters. Aunt Lily had even put a marshmallow in it, and used real chocolate, but I couldn't drink it. I put it down on the bench and walked to my bedroom, but when I got there, I couldn't remember what I'd gone there for, so I went to the lounge room. Aunt Lily was watching TV.

'I'm going to feed the chooks,' I told her as I walked right through the room and out to the hall.

'What? Why? I fed them this morning,' she said.

'I'll just check they're okay in this wind.'

'The chooks? Really?' She turned the TV off. 'Lainie, wait. Come here.'

With impatient steps I came back and picked up the remote. If she wasn't going to let me go outside, maybe I could watch something.

'What's going on?' she asked. 'Are you just upset about the Tatura Show or is there something else? You've been pacing around the house like a weaned calf. Ten minutes ago you flipped through all the TV channels and decided there was nothing good to watch and now you're doing it again. Why so restless?'

'Dunno. It's nothing, I guess. I've just got this nagging feeling. Like when you've seen something before. What's that called again?'

'Déjà vu?'

'Yeah. But it won't go away.'

I went over to the window and pulled back the curtain. The wind was throwing things around the farm like its parents had just banned it from watching TV. In a fit of temper, the storm had already chucked around buckets and horse rugs and empty chook feed bags and had torn Aunt Lily's jeans off the washing line and tipped over my old plastic wading pool. But it refused to rain, as if it was still too cranky to cry. I watched as a huge branch fell from one of the trees near the river. For such a heavy piece of wood, it travelled a long way before it hit the ground.

It looked dangerous out there. No one should be outside in this.

I turned back to my aunt. 'Noah's mum said she was dropping Noah home and then heading into town after she left here, right?'

'Yes. I think she was planning to do some shopping while Nicole's practice match was on.'

'Do you think they'd be home yet?'

Aunt Lily took the remote from me and turned the telly off again.

'Probably not yet, no. I'm sure they'll be back before dark though. Are you worried about her driving home in this wind?'

'What? No. Why would I be worried about Mrs Ashbree driving home? Is Noah's dad still in Melbourne?'

'Yes, until Thursday. Liam and Caleb are around though. What's bothering you, Lainie?'

I looked outside again, but the window was facing the wrong way so I walked into the kitchen and looked out towards the ridge where the tree tops were thrashing about. Dark clouds were trying to gather, but the wind was dispersing them too fast to form. I wished the storm would just hurry up and break. No one should be out there.

'Why would anyone be out there?' my aunt asked. I hadn't realised I'd said that out loud.

'Looking for treasure,' I said, feeling a bit sick.

'*What?*'

'Nothing. I don't know. It's just... Noah gave me this look as he was leaving. Caleb would notice if he went out on his dirt bike, wouldn't he?'

'Went where?' Aunt Lily looked alarmed now. She stood with me by the window. 'You think Noah's out there somewhere?'

I shrugged. Why would he be? I was being stupid. I told her so, but she picked up the phone. It rang for a long time before she gave up and hung it up. Then she went to the back door and put on her coat and boots. 'I'm going to talk to Harry.'

I followed her out, because I couldn't stay still. Were the twins out looking for Noah? Was that why they didn't answer the phone?

Chapter 6

Just a couple of minutes later I was sitting next to Harry in his ute, the satellite phone nestled in the console. Aunt Lily had taken her car over to the Ashbrees and was going to call us if Noah was there, but Harry had insisted that the two of us go straight out to the park to look.

We bumped along the rough track, taking the shortcut through our back paddocks that led straight out to a fire access trail and down to one of the old bridges.

Sticks and branches pelted the roof of the car but there was still no rain. The clouds were building rapidly though, making it seem very dark suddenly. Everything was tinged with a greenish glow.

Harry took one last look at the sky before we drove under the canopy of the cranky gum trees.

'Ice in those clouds,' he said. 'Let me know where we need to turn off.'

We drove on, dodging falling branches. The wind seemed calmer in amongst the scrub, but it was an illusion because above us the storm was tearing the bush apart, searching for us. It made me feel like hiding under the seat, like I had a massive secret to keep and didn't want anyone to see me. Harry was looking very grim, whispering under his breath in another language and I wondered if he was swearing at Noah in the language of his ancestors so I couldn't understand. Or maybe he was casting some mysterious ancient spell to try to settle the storm. If he was, it wasn't working.

At last we crossed the river, ancient fat wooden sleepers pounding rhythmically under our wheels, and I craned my neck to watch the water for as long as I could. It still swirled along, unaffected by the violence and chaos of the rest of the world. It would swallow up all the fallout from this storm and every other, turning all the debris into a part of its song and recycling it back into its story.

After a few more minutes, Harry spoke up.

'Noah fixed his dirt bike?'

'Yeah, but it's not very reliable.'

'I think I see a tyre track, but it's a bit too dark to follow easily.'

I peered over the bonnet but couldn't see anything. My stomach churned. If Harry could see it, then it was really happening. My best friend was out here somewhere and it was getting dark, and very cold, and there was ice in the clouds.

'He's over to the right of us,' I said, choosing not to dwell on why I felt so sure of that. 'But I don't think we can drive through that way. The bush looks too thick for a car.'

'Okay, I know a track that can get us farther north and then we can come back towards the river again. He must be somewhere in between, but first we need to help someone else.'

I blinked at him, hoping for more but he pretended not to notice. Harry wasn't one for volunteering any information he didn't want to share and I'd long since stopped trying to nag him, unless it was important, but I figured I'd find out soon enough.

A few minutes later we turned down a small cutaway that I'd never even noticed before. It didn't seem to lead anywhere at all but just a few metres down the not-meant-to-even-be-a-track, the police Landcruiser was parked, tilted at an awkward angle. The left front tyre was flat.

'Need a hand, sergeant?' Harry asked as he stepped out of the ute. He went straight for the tyre iron that lived under his seat, and in less than a minute he was on his knees looking for the best spot to place the jack that Sergeant Loxwood had been putting together.

'I didn't think I was driving over anything too sharp but I guess something punctured the side of the tyre,' the policeman said. 'I was afraid I was going to be stuck out in this storm for ages changing it. Thanks, Harry.'

The two of them swapped the flat in record time, which was good because Noah was still out there somewhere and he was an idiot and I was going to kill him for scaring me.

'So you're heading back to town now?' Harry asked the sergeant as they packed up.

'Yeah. There's nothing to see out here. Is there, Lainie?'

'I never said there was.'

He looked at me for a moment with his hands on his hips, waiting, but I had nothing else to say, so he turned back to Harry.

'This storm is getting worse. Do you want me to follow you back?'

'Nah, Mick, we'll be fine. We were just making sure the far gate was shut. Last storm we had, a tree came down on the hill paddock fence and we spent the next three days rounding up sheep out in the park. Now we shut all the external gates just in case. You head back to the road and we'll take the short cut back to our place.'

It didn't explain why we'd come this far out into the state park though. Why wasn't he telling the sergeant about Noah? For that matter, why hadn't I? Noah was in enough trouble with the policeman already. If Harry wasn't worried enough to get the sergeant involved, then I was happy to keep my mouth shut too. Sergeant Loxwood didn't question his explanation, which didn't surprise me much because everyone trusted Harry. Those deep brown eyes of his made me feel like nothing could ever go wrong with him around.

As the Landcruiser disappeared around a bend, some of that weird déjà vu feeling went with it and I let out a massive sigh of relief. I didn't like the idea of people wandering around out in the bush, murderers or policemen…or best friends. Harry got back in the ute and waited for me to climb in too.

'Lucky we came across him, don't you think, Lainie? And lucky for him he got the flat before he left the tracks. He should know better than to go driving off-road on his own.'

'Like we're about to do?'

He gave me a half smile and turned on the engine.

'You are weird, Harry. And a bit creepy, did anyone ever tell you that?'

'You have the same heritage as I do, you know. Maybe I should teach you some of the language.'

'So I can swear without anyone understanding me too?'

He laughed. 'Swear words are precious, powerful things. Don't waste them. What's the point of them if no one understands you?'

By the time I'd finished pondering that statement, it felt weird to ask any more questions about the sergeant's convenient flat tyre, and I was fretting too much about Noah to care that much anyway.

It was very slow going, driving in the ruts. The ute bottomed out a lot, and the track Harry found was so overgrown that we kept having to get out and move fallen logs out of our way. Once we even had to do some exploring to see which way to push through the scrub before the track reappeared. Just as we got back in the car, the rain started.

Great big splats of water hit the windscreen like bullets, and it was hard for Harry to hear what Aunt Lily was saying on the other end of the phone, but his expression stayed grim, so it wasn't the news I was hoping for.

'Leave it to me, Lily. You can trust me with this,' he said, and his voice was so soothing that I relaxed my grip on the door handle. He hung up and resumed driving, peering through the gloom in an effort to stay on the greasy track, or what remained of it. There were no more ruts here because no one ever came this far and I wondered if the last people to drive along here had been those murderers. I gripped the door handle again.

Soon it was dusk, at least where we were, on the eastern side of the ridge, hidden under a thick canopy of trees. Harry turned east again and the terrain changed, getting steeper as the land dropped down towards the river. There was no longer any track to follow but Harry kept pushing through until the ute began to slide sideways. My heart was in my mouth as he turned the wheel to head straight down the hill, making the car speed up, but I felt it gain traction again and as soon as we levelled out a little, he managed to stop.

He looked at me sideways. 'I'll walk from here,' he said calmly as if we hadn't just been about to end up as a pile of twisted metal and bones in the bottom of the gully.

I started to open the door, but he grabbed my elbow.

'You'll stay here,' he commanded. 'I promise I can find him on my own.'

Icy wind and rain invaded the car as he got out, sucking all the heat away, but there was no way I was turning the engine back on just to make the heater work. In fact, the ute rocked so much when Harry slammed his door shut that I was afraid the handbrake wouldn't hold, and that it would start sliding again. I peered down the hill but Harry had turned off the headlights so all I could see was that it dropped away into what was probably not the gorge filled with lava that my brain was imagining. Rain turned to hail, millions of balls of ice bouncing off the bonnet and carpeting the slope in front of the wheels. Millions of near frictionless balls…

I tried to follow Harry really quietly, but he was waiting for me under a cape wattle, shaking his head. We walked on in silence, hurrying as best we could through patches of wattle and prickly heath bushes. The hailstorm passed, briefly, and then hit us again with renewed violence and I cowered against Harry as we waited it out under a rivergum that did very little to help shelter us.

'I think he's closer to the river now,' I yelled over the noise of the hail. 'Down that way.' I pointed towards a shadowy outcrop that loomed out across the hill in the distance, and Harry nodded. As soon as the hail settled again we kept going, until Harry paused at a large bush with red flowers on it. In the remaining glow I could just see that one of its branches was freshly broken, and below it was a distinctive gouge in the dirt, with the imprint of a tyre tread. We followed the trail down the hill, zig-zagging from time to time when it got too steep. The hail had turned to rain again, and I was shivering so much I could barely walk straight. I kept blinking water from my eyes but not fast enough to stop me tripping over Noah's dirt bike when it suddenly appeared under my feet. Harry managed to grab my shoulder just in time.

'Noah?' I called, but I knew he wasn't nearby.

Harry leant down to feel the engine. 'Cold,' he said. 'Completely.' Then he peered closer at the handlebars, and wiped his fingers against them.

'Is that blood?' I asked, horrified. I didn't even let him answer, but ran down the hill towards the bluff. What had Noah been thinking, coming out here on his own?

'Lainie, wait!'

No. I wasn't going to wait.

'Stop running, it's too slippery! Why do you never…'

I could hear him following, and grumbling, but most of his words lost themselves in the wind.

'…should send you to live next door,' he grouched. I guess he thought Mrs Ashbree could discipline me better, and he was probably right but I didn't care. Noah was hurt somewhere and it was my fault. I had to get to him. The hill became steep enough that there were hardly any bushes left to trip over but it also became rockier. Loose stones rolled beneath my feet a few times but I always managed to recover my balance. Heavy rain tried to wash me down into the river. I ignored it. Noah needed me more than the river did right now.

'Noah!' I called as loudly as I could with my chest heaving. The shadowy outcrop turned out to be part of a rocky bluff that marked where the ground fell away towards the river. Like the bones of the hill were sticking out and the flesh under it had all crumbled away. 'Noah, I'm coming!'

I fought my way through some bushes that sat above the outcrop and then headed downhill again until I found a way to climb up onto it.

The rocks felt rough under my frozen fingers and my boots had good grip. I could hear Harry calling my name so I called back to him, but didn't stop. When I reached a level spot I stood up, balancing one hand against the rock above me while I looked around. If Noah had been hoping to find shelter up here he would have been disappointed, although it looked like there might be a bit of an overhang farther along. I stepped over a deep crevice filled with runoff from the temporary waterfalls above me, and then jumped up to the next boulder. Some loose rocks came away under my fingers as I reached for the one after that. I managed to hold on, wriggling on my belly until I was sprawled over the top of it. Another deep crevice lay below me, filled with fallen rocks and debris, and among it all was the body of my best friend, lying in the hail. Was he even alive? I could barely see him in the gloom. Something looked very wrong with the way his right arm was sticking out. It looked like he'd tried to jump the gap to reach the overhang for some shelter. How was I supposed to get to him? I kept calling to him, but he didn't move. What if he was dead? Because of my stupid obsession over that newspaper clipping? I blinked water from my eyes that wasn't all rain and wriggled over to my left, where a small rock gave me a bit of a step down. From there I couldn't see any way to get closer.

'Lainie, stop moving,' Harry called from above me. He still sounded calm. Nothing ever fazed him. He must have found a way to climb the opposite side of the outcrop because he was on the far side of the crevice, under the overhang. He was using the torch he'd grabbed from his glovebox to inspect the rocks, looking for a safe way down.

I crouched where I was, shivering and angry. Why had Noah come out here? He didn't even believe me about the diamonds. I peered down at him, trying to see if his chest was moving, but he was too far away and it was too dark. All I could see was how pale his face looked in the gloom. Even his blond hair was dark when it was so wet.

'I need you to stay where you are,' Harry told me. 'Everything will be fine but we have to be careful and take our time.' He looked at me for a long moment, as if trying to decide something, and then he turned and looked to the north, and let out a big sigh.

'Harry, we can't take too long,' I called through the rain. 'The police will take hours to get here – if they can find us at all. I know you have rope in the ute, but where would we even tie it? I think – '

Harry tucked the torch into his back pocket and slid down the series of rocks, agile as a possum, landing in the crevice without so much as a stumble. A few small rocks skittered away, the sound of their passage lost in the wind and rain. He squatted down next to Noah, blocking my view, and I couldn't breathe. *Please be alive, please be alive...*

I jumped a bit when the torch came back on again, and watched impatiently while the farmhand inspected Noah from head to toe. Then he rolled him onto his side.

'Noah, mate, wake up.' Harry's voice was the eye of the storm. A safe haven in amongst the chaos. 'If you can wake up, we can get you home much sooner,' he crooned. 'Back in your own bed. Home with your family.'

Listen to him, Noah. Wake up.

'Come on, Noah. You can do this,' Harry continued with calm determination. 'It might hurt for a while but it's better to face the pain now. Trust me. The longer you try to avoid it, the worse it will get. Wake up.'

Was that movement? It was so dark now. And so cold. How long had he been lying there?

Harry stripped off his oilskin jacket and then his shirt, but didn't stop talking. 'Noah, I won't let anything happen to you, I promise.' He tucked the jacket under Noah's head, and then took his face in his hands, as if it would somehow force him to listen. 'I can take you home.'

Something about the way he said 'home' settled in my chest with a soft bump. The word seemed to be filled with so much meaning. Comfort and healing and warmth and family...and something more. Something tantalising, mysterious...

At last I saw Noah stir. With a quiet sob of relief I flopped down on my tiny ledge and tucked my knees up to my chest to squeeze down my violent shivering. Noah was alive, so that left just the freezing rain as the cause of my shaking.

'There's a pretty deep cut below his ribs,' Harry called up to me as he tore a strip from the shirt to press against it. 'I expect that's where the blood on the bike came from. I can't see any head wounds but there must be a reason he was unconscious so we'll have to be very careful.' The rest of the shirt was used to tie his broken arm to his chest and then Harry zipped up his waterproof jacket over the top. The whole time I just watched from above, too angry at Noah to speak. He probably didn't even know I was there. In fact he looked so out of it that I wasn't even sure he knew Harry was there.

'I'll lift him back up towards you,' Harry called. 'It looks like an easier climb.'

'How can I help?'

'Take the torch,' he said, tossing it up to me. My wet fingers scrambled but I caught it okay. Then I shone it at the rock face below me, trying to give him the best possible visibility for his climb.

With Noah clinging as best he could to his back, Harry lifted them both slowly up the side of the crevice. It reminded me of when we were very little and Harry used to carry us in from the river so we wouldn't get bindii prickles in our feet. That was a long time ago. Noah was a lot heavier now – I could testify to that from when he'd tackled me in footy at lunchtime the previous week – but Harry made it look easy. The man was not exactly heavy-set but I'd seen him lift wet sheep and unload full truckloads of hay. Nothing would ever be too much for him to handle.

'There's a better rock to your right,' I told him. 'Yep, that one. And you can put your left foot on that little one there maybe.' I shone the torchlight to the one I meant. 'Here, I'll get back up so you can use this ledge and have a bit of a rest.'

The hail started up again, and something came out of Harry's mouth that almost sounded like a swear word, but couldn't have been, because it was Harry. Other farmers always made jokes about how he never swore. I put the torch in my mouth and carefully stood up. My legs were so numb. I heard Harry say something else but the hail was too loud so I just concentrated on trying to climb. I hooked my right hand over the boulder and swung my leg up after it, just finding a foothold with the edge of my boot. When I finally leant over the top of the rock, I spat out the poor torch.

'It's only a short lift up from the ledge,' I called back to Harry.

'What?'

I turned a little further to face him. 'I said, it's only a short – '

Something gave way under my fingers, and I grabbed at the boulder but all I could feel were tiny balls of ice and then it felt like the whole rock face just disappeared. For a couple of seconds I was part of the hailstorm, just another blob of heavenly debris hurtling towards the Earth. And then I wasn't. All the breath left my lungs as my left shoulder landed…somewhere, and I couldn't breathe in again. Rocks slid under me, and I curled up a bit to protect my head, waiting for everything to stop. It didn't. It all moved faster. Ice and rock and water pulled me downwards and everything was sharp and hard. I wanted to dig in my heels and try to stop but I couldn't seem to get my legs to notice any signals other than the pain from all the new bruises my knees were collecting. My fingers grabbed at rock after rock, all of which came loose to join the game. Finally, I managed to grab something solid. A dry bush of some sort, holding tenaciously to the pockets of dirt that had collected between the long fallen stones. My body swung down below it, with my bruised hip coming to rest on a jutting out root. For a few seconds I just kept as still as I could, not even daring to think in case it changed something. I just wanted everything to stay perfectly still…

'Lainie!'

I heard Harry bellow, his usually calm voice sounding harsh and broken as it cut through the night. I couldn't answer. Not yet. Too winded. I'd played enough footy to know what it felt like to get winded, so I didn't panic. Then I wondered why I wasn't panicking. Then I worried about the fact that I was thinking too much and that might make something move. *Then* I panicked. The slope I was lying on didn't feel too steep, but when I tried to get my feet under me I couldn't. They seemed to be dangling in thin air.

Don't do it, Lainie. Don't look. I looked, and could see nothing. No moonlight reflected from the slope below me because there *was* no slope below me. End of the line. The ground fell away and whatever fell with it wasn't likely to connect with anything until it splashed into the river far below. There were still some small rocks and hailstones rolling past me to show how that was done. I held onto the trunk of the bush with a death grip, closed my eyes and tried to get my lungs to work. On the plus side, I no longer felt cold. My body was a mix of numb parts and very sore parts, but I was not cold.

'Lainie, don't try to move. I'll come down and get you,' Harry called, still sounding far too calm. How did he even know I hadn't fallen right off the cliff? 'I need to get Noah somewhere a bit safer and then I'll come down for you.'

It made sense, but I didn't like it. Very slowly I reached up and grabbed the little trunk with my other hand as well, like it was a scrawny neck that I wanted to strangle very, very gently. It showered me with tiny dead leaves and a few twigs as a reward. Not so much a healthy, living bush, then. Wonderful.

The hail stopped again, finally, and everything went quiet. Fresh rivulets gurgled above me as the rainwater answered the call of the river below. If I answered its call too, would I learn its secrets? Find its source? When I was young my aunt used to tell me stories of magical creatures that lived by the water. Were there elves hiding down there, in the Barramundi Triangle, calling to me? Maybe I should join them like my dad had, all those years ago. Had he been scared? Or had it all happened way too fast for him too? Were there no dead bushes for him to cling to? Not even one?

Apparently it was still possible to cry when you were winded. Dad's accident felt far too real all of a sudden. I couldn't remember being told what had happened. It felt like I'd always known. I was only three so had no memory of the incident itself – I must have asked my aunt about it at some point. Then I stopped asking because I didn't want to re-live it over and over, but now…now it was in my face, unavoidable. Every thought he might have had, every feeling, every physical experience of bruising and pain. The fear that warred with the irrational confidence that said pure determination would make everything okay again. The unexpected calm and logic that would have prevailed once he embraced the panic and moved through to the other side. I'd always wondered what it must have been like. Now I knew.

My arms were aching badly, and everything started to shake again. Even though I couldn't feel the cold any more, I was drenched in icy rain from head to toe and very tired. I wouldn't be able to hold on for long, but Harry wasn't going to be able to move very fast, carrying Noah up the side of the crevice.

Soft rain caressed my hair like a gentle hand, coaxing me to relax and let go. Instead I began to concentrate harder on my grip. I squeezed a little harder with my right hand so I could relax my left one for a few seconds, then I swapped over. It wasn't enough to stop my right one from cramping up, so I let go for just a second to shake it out. When I grabbed at the trunk again, something moved and I slipped a few inches further. A root had broken, and my face got showered with old crumbly dirt. I stopped crying in that instant, still struggling to breathe. *Harry, please don't take too long!*

Blinking away the dirt, I noticed the torchlight scanning the slope above me, searching. So Harry had at least made it to the boulder where I'd left it. I knew he couldn't leave Noah there; it wasn't big enough, or flat enough.

'I'm down further,' I tried to call, but my voice had no power in it. I needed him to know where the drop-off was before he ended up like my dad. 'Harry, be careful, it gets much steeper – '

As I lifted my head up to project my feeble voice better, another root broke, and the whole bush swung around, dangling only by a tiny side root. I had seconds left. There was no way it could hold me. Pressing my knees into the dirt I started to scramble, wriggling upwards as best I could, hoping to get high enough to find something for my feet to grip onto. Pebbles and dirt and ice rolled beneath me and I felt like I was trying to run up a downwards escalator. My right arm searched above me for something to hold, but everything kept coming away in my fingers.

Light shone in my eyes, drawn by the sound of clattering stones, and I looked right into it like a startled possum. Then the light disappeared. My hands and elbows stung as I squirmed. It was hard to tell if I was getting anywhere. Still I fought, wanting to scream but not having enough breath to do it with. A bigger rock rolled past me, hitting me on the shoulder, so I knew I had started the landslide again. Skin split as my knees scraped against stone and I welcomed it because it was better than feeling nothing to push against, like my feet and shins. Any second now, I was going to run out of slope. How was Harry supposed to get to me without getting caught in this death trap? He couldn't. There was no way.

Maybe I should stop him trying.

If I just let go, he would see, and he would stay where it was safe, screaming at the sky like they did in the movies. If I just let go.

Then what? Aunt Lily would be alone, and Noah would blame himself and never fool around again, and I would have my own newspaper clipping, and everyone would think that Noah and I had been doing something dumb and they'd be right...

I wriggled like I had never wriggled before, scrambling against the rocky tide, moving faster than it did and not touching anything for long enough for it to disappear from under me. Everything hurt. I'd been sensible and held on for as long as I could but if I didn't rescue myself now, I'd be lost. There was no way Harry could get to me in time. My hand found something that held for just a few seconds before it came away, long enough to gain a few precious centimetres. I dug my left knee into a patch of mud, and pushed hard, and then felt my right shin hit the edge or the drop-off. So that's where it was. That meant my left foot must almost be close to it too. Another push, with everything, all at once, and I felt my boot touch, and so I pushed again as hard as I could.

For a few moments it got a bit easier; the slope didn't seem so steep when I could use all four limbs. Rocks were still bouncing all around me. Then something hit me below the eye, making me flinch but I didn't dare stop moving. I headed over to my left where there was less debris, and found a small protruding boulder to cling to. The cold wet granite was a cuddly as a teddy bear. Mr Bunji. I named it and hugged it and promised to love it forever all in the space of about half a second.

Mr Bunji held me and I held him, and he let me cry on him and didn't complain. I was not going to die. For a few seconds I couldn't do anything except tremble and cling and cry. Then I remembered Harry. I made myself suck in enough breath to be heard.

'I'm okay. Stay up there,' I called. 'It's far too unstable down here; you'll only make things worse.'

The torchlight appeared again, and I could see Harry halfway down the crevice, below where Noah had been. He was using the rocks along the side to steady himself, but he would have struggled to get much farther without getting caught on the scree. The light shone in my eyes again as he inspected my situation.

'Are you hurt?' he asked.

'Just bruises, and still a bit winded.' But alive. Unexpectedly alive.

'There's a bit of a plateau just above you where you can rest. Want me to come around and get you?'

I pushed a tangle of muddy hair out of my eyes and then followed the torchlight to see the spot he meant. It was simple to get to. After what I'd just done, that bit looked so, so *simple*.

My voice was crazy shaky. 'No, I can do it. Thanks, Harry.'

'Anytime, Lainie-bug.'

***

Neither of us spoke a word after he crushed me into a fierce bear hug when we met above the bluff. There wasn't anything to say. He looked me over with the torchlight, and checked my pupils. They reacted just fine when he shone the torch straight into them, so without another word, he slung Noah over his shoulder again and began the trek back to the ute. By the time we got there, Noah was very sleepy. I still didn't think he realised I was there because no one was really in the mood for talking.

I waited until Harry had reversed back up the hill before I climbed into the tray and huddled under the tarp with the toolbox. It wasn't quite as cuddly as Mr Bunji, especially when it tried to climb into my lap every time we hit a good bump.

When we finally made it home, Noah was fast asleep but not unconscious, and Mrs Ashbree was waiting to take him straight to Nalong Hospital. I crawled out of the tray and into my aunt's arms, and after she'd put me in a hot shower and poured warm Milo down my throat, she sat on the end of my bed. Just in case I wanted to talk. And I did.

Chapter 7

On Monday afternoon I sat cross-legged on the end of Noah's hospital bed, unwrapping a chocolate for him. Mrs Ashbree had bought me a huge box for raising the alarm. She didn't know anything about my near death experience, and neither did Noah, and they were never going to find out so long as Harry and my aunt kept their promises.

'But how did Harry even find me?' Noah asked.

'I guess he has some cool aboriginal tracking skills we didn't know about,' I hedged, wondering the same thing. We'd gone pretty much straight to the right place, maybe because of Sergeant Loxwood's description. He'd mentioned that my mother had helped the police find the spot by following the river, so we'd known roughly where Noah would have headed...that must have been it.

'Yeah, he certainly seems to have more indigenous blood than you do. Not that you'll listen to him about those sacred marked tree stories.'

'Hey, did you hand in your essay?'

He scrunched up his cheek. 'I forgot. It's done, though,' he said defensively. 'I think it's inside my maths book, in your locker.'

'Why on earth would it be in...?' Then I remembered. 'That might be a problem,' I said, tugging my lower lip.

Noah picked idly at the bandage on his chest and shrugged. 'I'm going home tonight, and Mum said I can come to school tomorrow. I'll just hand it in then.'

'That's not it,' I said. 'But you do have a pretty good excuse for an extension, if they believe your book really was in my locker.'

One blond eyebrow asked me why.

'Because some idiot set my locker on fire over the weekend.'

Noah sat up straighter. 'What for?'

I bit into a heart-shaped chocolate filled with pink goo. 'Who knows why Ben does anything? I swear, he's the bane of my life. I think he needs some sort of psych assessment. Maybe he'll get one now.'

'How can you be certain it was him?'

'Because he told Jake, who bragged about it to everyone at recess, and Tessa dobbed him in.'

Noah looked like he wanted to start ranting about him, which, if he had to write his whole essay again, was only fair, but I wasn't in the mood so I changed the topic.

'Harry went and got your dirt bike yesterday. He says you busted the gudgeon pin. Noah, why the hokey did you stay out there for so long once the weather turned? It's not like there was anything to find out there. Even if you'd just come back to the track we could have come and got you much sooner. Did you get lost?'

He fiddled with the foil from the chocolate with his one good hand. 'I thought I *was* heading back to the track, but somehow I kept getting drawn north, back to the river. I guess my subconscious was trying to take me straight home, even though that wasn't the fastest way. Then I got skewered by that branch so I kept away from the trees and then the bike cut out on me. I'm sorry I was so stupid, not telling anyone where I was going. I just wanted to get some answers for you. About your mum.'

'I did get answers, Noah. I pestered Harry until he caved and told me. There are no diamonds, and my mum…I guess she was just like us. She stuck her nose in where she shouldn't have and got herself in trouble, but it all worked out fine.'

Noah looked out the window to the west, and the darkening sky. 'No secrets hidden out in the Barramundi Triangle, then?'

From the hospital window we could barely make out the line of trees that marked the ridge. Too many buildings in the way.

'No, Noah. Nothing out there but the trees, the rabbits, a few rock wallabies and the singing river.'

'Yeah,' he mumbled, his eyes thoughtful. 'But whose song does it sing?'

Songlines
(The Sentinels of Eden, Book One)

Available August 20, 2016

We belong to the Earth, Lainie-Bug. We were sent here in human form for a reason. If you don't know what to do, then just be human.

Right. Like that was ever a simple thing to do.

In the heart of the Wimmera region of Victoria, an ancient gateway to Eden is kept hidden and safe by a creature so powerful that even the moon would obey her commands — at least it would if she had any idea that she wasn't just a normal girl about to finish high school.

When a mining company begins exploratory sampling near Lainie's sheep farm, a family secret is revealed that makes her regret not having learnt more about her Indigenous heritage.

What she's told by their farmhand, Harry – an Aboriginal Elder – can't possibly be true, but then the most irritating guy in class, Bane, begins to act even more insanely toward her than ever, until she can no longer deny that something very unusual is going on.

When Harry doesn't return from his quest to seek help to protect the area from the miners, Lainie sets out to discover the truth of her heritage, and of the secret she's been born to protect.

Available 20th August 2016 from <u>Odyssey Books</u> (<u>www.odysseybooks.com.au</u>) or <u>The Bentonet</u> (thebentonet.com.au) or the usual e-book retailers.

To find out more or connect with Carolyn Denman visit her website: <u>carolyndenman.com</u>, Facebook: <u>Carolyn J Denman</u>, Good Reads Profile: <u>Carolyn Denman</u> or follow on Twitter: @ <u>CDenmanAuthor.</u>

www.ingramcontent.com/pod-product-compliance
Lightning Source LLC
Chambersburg PA
CBHW020144150626
46552CB00021B/1665